# Let's Dance!

George Ancona

Morrow Junior Books    *New York*

If you can speak, you can sing.
If you can walk, you can dance.
All you have to do is

kick,

step,

turn,

hop,

reach,

jump,

leap,

and wiggle.

# Fast or slow?
# Listen to
# the music.

SAXOPHONE

SCOTTISH BAGPIPES

TIBETAN FIDDLE

The rhythm
will tell you
how to move.

CONGOLESE DRUM

You can dance alone,

SCOTTISH COUNTRY DANCERS. This dance developed in the Lowlands of Scotland and was influenced by early French, Italian, and English dancing. The footwork is complicated and lively.

with a friend,

or with a whole bunch of people.

CIRCLE FOLK
DANCE.
Young people at
a summer camp
join hands in a
joyful unrehearsed
dance.

AFGHAN WEDDING DANCE.
In Afghanistan, a dancer holds a saucer in each hand to wish the bride and groom good fortune.

Dancing is a way of celebrating.

CHINESE LION DANCE. This dance is performed to celebrate the New Year to the accompaniment of crashing cymbals and bursting firecrackers.

There are dances that celebrate the seasons.

ENGLISH MORRIS DANCERS perform during a springtime ceremony. The bells on their feet are to wake up the earth so it will receive the seeds in the spring planting.

PUEBLO HARVEST DANCE. In the fall, Native Americans of the Southwest pueblos celebrate the season with a dance that gives thanks for a good harvest.

SEVILLANAS. A flamenco dance from Spain with Gypsy and Moorish origins. The guitarists are accompanied by singers who also clap to accentuate the rhythm of the music.

# Dances from the old countries

THE JARANA is a dance from the Yucatan peninsula of Mexico. It is a blend of Spanish and native Mayan rhythms. The women wear white *huipiles* with colorful embroidery. The men dress all in white.

were brought to the New World.

People dress up
to dance in their
traditional clothes.

GREEK FOLK DANCERS

POWWOW FANCY DANCER

POLYNESIAN DANCER

MATACHINE DANCER

KOREAN FAN DANCER

MEXICAN HAT DANCERS

# Children dance in their parents' footsteps.

PUEBLO HARVEST DANCE

CONTRA DANCE

# Over time, dances change.

CLOG DANCING originated in northern England, where miners would dance with their wooden shoes. Their descendants who settled in the Appalachian mountains continued the tradition.

TAP DANCING developed from clog dancing. It mixes Irish, English, African, and Native American styles together. Instead of clogs, tap dancers wear shoes with metal taps on the heels and toes.

# There are dances for men

POLYNESIAN WAR DANCE. As in many cultures, the warriors of Polynesia—the islands of the Pacific—dance in preparation for battle.

# and dances for women.

TURKISH GYPSY FOLK DANCE. A playful dance that celebrates women's strength. The women tap finger cymbals as they dance and tease the audience.

# Animals dance.

TIBETAN YAK DANCE.
The noble yak provides milk, clothing, and transportation for Tibetans. Two men wear a yak costume and dance to poke fun at humans.

# Puppets dance.

MEXICAN PUPPETS are carried by little boys who dance for the entertainment of children at birthday parties. The puppets are made by the town's piñata maker.

# There are country dances

CONTRA DANCING was called country dancing in England. Dancers switch partners as they move up and down the line. Families gather at BARN DANCES to dance the Texas two-step.

**and city dances.**

BREAK DANCING began on the streets and playgrounds of the inner cities. Young men try to outdo each other with acrobatic movements to hip-hop music.

# There are dances that tell stories.

CLASSIC NORTH INDIAN DANCES tell stories. The dancers depict the characters of a story with mime—changes of facial expressions and poses.

One day, the jealous god Indra demanded that the villagers bring him the offerings they were taking to the god Krishna. Old and young, the villagers followed his orders.

Krishna appeared and told the villagers to bring him the gifts as they always did.

When Indra heard of this, he became very angry and shot his arrows into the sky, which caused rain and lightning to appear.

The rains soon flooded the village and the mountain. People tried to swim away from the rising waters.

Krishna appeared. He raised the mountain on his pinkie and saved the people and the village.

# Some dances are performed on stage.

THE NUTCRACKER BALLET is a Christmas story about a little girl who gets a magic nutcracker that turns into a prince. He takes her to a magic land of dancers, snowflakes, and sugarplum fairies.

WHEELCHAIR DANCING enables people with physical disabilities to perform. Their joy is shared with their audience.

And even if you can't walk, you can still dance.

# Most people dance to have fun

and to share happy feelings.

# to Catherine Oppenheimer

*Thanks* to the many dancers and friends who helped make this book possible: Caroline Oppenheimer, Sam Shankman and David Prouty of the National Dance Institute, the Swat Team, and the kids of Tesuque Elementary School; Chris and Rujecko Berry, Titos Sampas, Dorjee Gyaltsen and the Potala Tibetan Dance Troupe, the Contra Dancers at the Odd Fellows Hall, Gisela Genschow of the Santa Fe Dance Foundation, Jewel Sato, Nyssia Choukour-Wali, Yamuna Wali, Rosario Betanzos-Gonzalez, Thayer Morris, Carla Populus and Pueblo Flamenco, Ruth Alpert and Tom Adler, Albuquerque Summer Fest, Chinese Dancers, Polynesian Dancers, MiGyung Brown of the Korean Chorus, Nick Lothetis and Mary Ann Kaye of the St. George Church Greek Dancers, Dancers Supporting Dancers, Desert Thistle Highland Dancers, Expresiones Academia de Artes Dancers, Myra Keen Morris, Baila, Baila Dancers, Santa Fe Fiesta Dancers, San Ildefonso Pueblo, Don Ricardo Nuñez Gijón, Polynesian Cultural Center, Charlene Curtiss and Joanne Petroff of Light Motion, Christopher Barela, Phillips Manor, Camp Farm & Wilderness, the Matachines of El Rancho, and to all the unknown dancers at the many festivals and gatherings I photographed. And to Michael "Link" Tate for suggesting the traditional African saying with which I begin this book.

Published by Morrow Junior Books a division of William Morrow and Company, Inc. 1350 Avenue of the Americas, New York, NY 10019 www.williammorrow.com

Printed in Hong Kong by South China Printing Company (1988) Ltd.

1 2 3 4 5 6 7 8 9 10

Library of Congress Cataloging-in-Publication Data
Ancona, George.
Let's dance/George Ancona.
p. cm.
Summary: Simple text and photographs describe various dances from all over the world.
ISBN 0-688-16211-8 (trade)—
ISBN 0-688-16212-6 (library)
1. Dance—Juvenile literature.   2. Folk dancing—Juvenile literature.   3. Dance—Pictorial works—Juvenile literature.   4. Folk dancing—Pictorial works—Juvenile literature.   [1. Folk dancing.   2. Dance.]
I. Title.  GV1596.5.A55 1998  793.3'1—dc21
97-52022   CIP  AC